LET'S PLAY CARDS!

To R. A. K. and J. M. S.—true card sharks.

—E. S.

This book is for Deanna & Philip, Katherine & Gail, Leepie & Peetie, Stevie & Blackie, Mayzie & Mia! Lots of huge THANK YOUs to Mikey, Julie, Lindley, Lee, Ann, Chani & Ruth!

—J. K.

First Aladdin Paperbacks Edition, 1996
Text copyright © 1996 by Elizabeth Silbaugh
Illustrations copyright © 1996 by Jef Kaminsky

Aladdin Paperbacks
An imprint of Simon & Schuster Children's Publishing Division
1230 Avenue of the Americas
New York, NY 10020

READY-TO-READ is a registered trademark of Simon & Schuster, Inc.
Also available in a Simon & Schuster Books for Young Readers Edition.

Manufactured in the United States of America
10 9 8 7 6 5 4 3 2 1

The Library of Congress has cataloged the Simon & Schuster Books for Young Readers Edition as follows:
Silbaugh, Elizabeth.
Let's Play Cards! : a first book of card games / by Elizabeth Silbaugh ;
illustrated by Jef Kaminsky.
p.   cm. — (Ready-to-Read)
Summary: Provides a simple introduction to playing cards and directions for the games of War, Concentration, Go Fish, Crazy Eights, and Clock Solitaire.
1. Card games—Juvenile literature. [1. Card games. 2. Games.]
I. Kaminsky, Jef, ill. II. Title. III. Series.
GV1244.S55   1996
795.4—dc20   96-596
CIP   AC
ISBN 0-689-80802-X (hc)   ISBN 0-689-80801-1 (pbk)

LET'S PLAY CARDS!

A FIRST BOOK OF CARD GAMES

By Elizabeth Silbaugh

Illustrated by Jef Kaminsky

Ready-to-Read

Aladdin Paperbacks

Outside, it's a cold, rainy night.
Inside, it's cozy and warm.
You are sipping cocoa.

What will you do for fun?
Suddenly, you have an idea.
"Let's play cards!"

Some card games are silly.

Some card games are serious.

You can play cards by yourself.

You can play cards with another person.
Or you can play cards in a group.
This book will get you started.
All you need is a little patience—
and a deck of cards!

Cool Carl the
Card Shark, here!
I'll add some POINTERS
from time to time!

Before you start playing,
you should know a few things.
A complete deck has 52 cards.
Thirteen of them are spades.
Thirteen of them are hearts.

Thirteen of them are diamonds.
Thirteen of them are clubs.
Spades, hearts, diamonds, and clubs
are called "suits."

Some decks have
an extra two cards.
These are the Jokers.
Jokers don't have suits.

9

Now take a look at the numbers
and letters on the cards.
In each suit, you will see
cards numbered from two to ten.
You will also see
four special cards in each suit.
Three of these are called "face cards."
The King is the highest.
The Queen comes next, then the Jack.
All the face cards are higher than
the cards with numbers.
The last special card is the Ace.
It has the letter A in the corners.

See the faces?
Not quite enough
teeth for my taste, but . . .
In some games, the Ace
is the highest card of all.
But in other games, the
Ace acts like a one.

11

To play most card games, you need to practice three things.

1. Shuffling the cards. Here are some good ways.

Pile-shuffle. Just dump the cards on the table and mix them around.

Cut-shuffle. Hold the pack in one hand. With the other hand, lift off a few cards and gently push them back into the rest of the pack.

Flutter-shuffle. Grasp half of the pack flat in each hand. Use your thumbs to flutter the two halves into each other.

2. Dealing the cards.
If you are the dealer, give a card face-down
to each player, starting on your left.
Give one to yourself last.
Always deal from
the top of the deck.

3. Holding the
cards in a fan.
The cards you are dealt
are called your "hand."
To keep other players from seeing what
you have, make a fan.
First, hold your cards in a pack;
then slide them around into a half circle.
Be sure to hold the fan up so
no one can peek!

Are you ready to start playing? Good!

You won't use
a fan here.

Game #1: WAR
Number of players: 2
Shuffle the cards and
deal out the whole deck.
Now you each have 26 cards.
Don't look at your cards.
Just hold them in a pack, face-down.

Touch the top card on your pack.
At the count of three,
flip the top card face-up onto the table.
Both players do this at the same time.

Is your card higher?
Yes! You win both cards!
Slide them onto the bottom
of your pack.
Keep flipping cards face-up
and seeing who wins.

By the way, in this game,
Jokers are the highest.
Aces are the next highest,
then the face cards.

17

Now for the tricky part.
What if the flipped cards are the same?
Let's say you both turned up Jacks.
It's time for a *War!*
Each of you deals three cards
face-down from the top of your pack.

At the count of three,
flip the fourth card face-up.
Whose is higher?
The winner takes all ten cards.

Snatched from
the jaws of defeat!

If those fourth cards are the same,
it's time for a *Double War!*
Both of you lay down three more cards.
Flip the fourth one face-up.
The winner takes all 18 cards!
To win a game of War,
you must get every card in the deck.

War can take a long time.
Pour some cocoa,
and have fun!

Do you know what "good
sportsmanship" is?
It is remembering
not to gloat too much.
We all win some;
we all lose some.

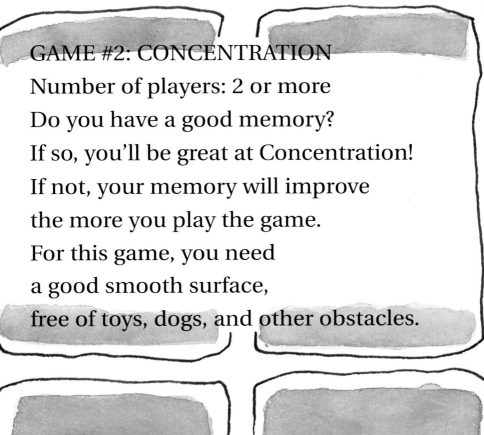

GAME #2: CONCENTRATION

Number of players: 2 or more

Do you have a good memory?

If so, you'll be great at Concentration!

If not, your memory will improve

the more you play the game.

For this game, you need

a good smooth surface,

free of toys, dogs, and other obstacles.

Start by shuffling the cards, as usual.
Then lay out the whole deck
face-down in rows.
When it is your turn,
flip over any two cards.
Do they make a pair?
A pair is two cards with
matching letters or numbers.
If you did not get a pair,
flip the cards back over.
That's the end of your turn.
If you *did* turn up a pair,
take the cards out of the rows.
Stash them away by your side.
You get to go again—right now.

No, no, no, you shrimp!
Not that kind of pear!

There are d'Anjou,
Bartlett, and many
other kinds of delicious
pears out there.

During other
players' turns,
try to concentrate
on which cards they flip over.
Your good memory will help you
on your next turn!

When all the cards have been taken,
count up your pairs.
You guessed it:
the player with the most cards wins.

Want to play again?
To make it harder, don't
lay the cards in an even grid.
Put them every which way.
Be sure to shuffle well,
and keep that playing surface clear.

You're doing
swimmingly!

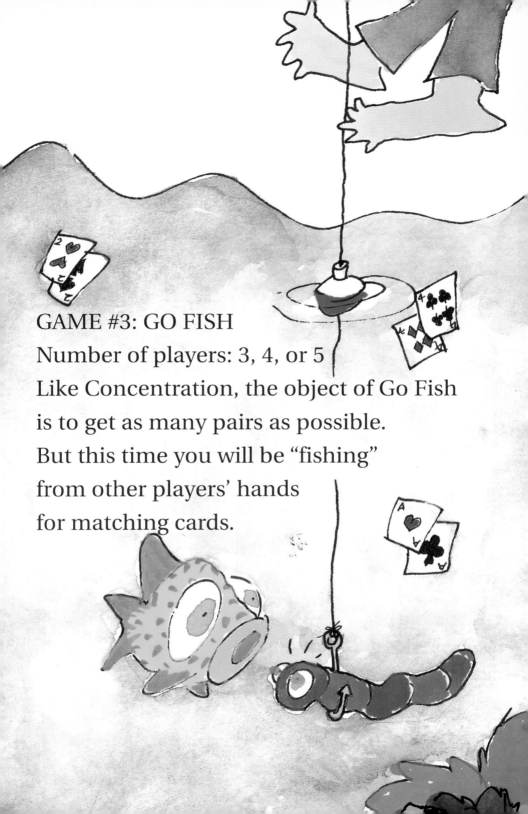

GAME #3: GO FISH
Number of players: 3, 4, or 5
Like Concentration, the object of Go Fish
is to get as many pairs as possible.
But this time you will be "fishing"
from other players' hands
for matching cards.

Deal five cards to each player.
The stack of leftover cards goes
in the middle of the table, face-down.
Hold your cards in a fan.
Do you see any pairs?

If you do, put them down
on the table in front of you.
If you do not, you will have to
wait your turn to "go fish."

Give that
kid a "hand"!

As the dealer, you go first.
Ask another player for a card
that matches one you already have.
For example, let's say
you have a Queen in your hand.
You would pick another player and ask,
"Molly, do you have a Queen?"

If Molly has the card,
she must hand it over.
Put your new pair down
in front of you.
Now you get to go again!
Pick any player and ask for
another card.
If the player you picked does
not have it,
he says, *"Go fish!"*
Then you must draw a card
from the stack.
This is the end of your turn.

If you happen to pick
the exact card you
were asking for,
take another turn!

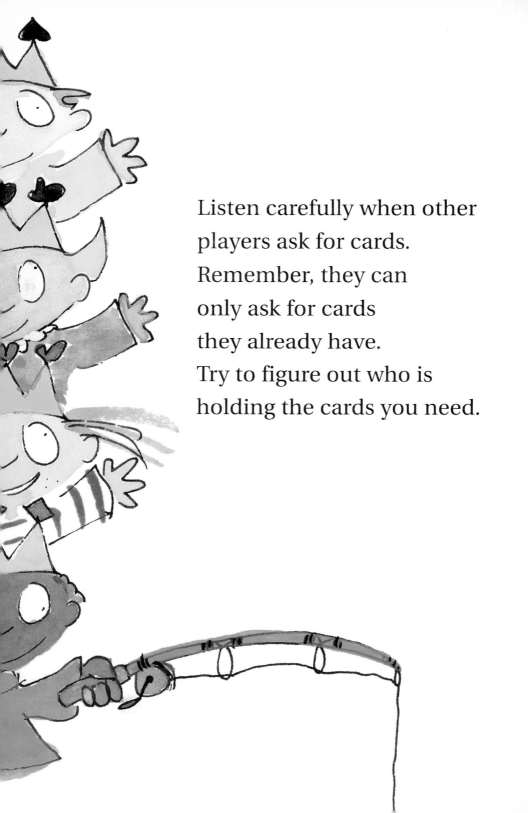

Listen carefully when other
players ask for cards.
Remember, they can
only ask for cards
they already have.
Try to figure out who is
holding the cards you need.

Then you will know where
to go fishing!
The game ends when any
player runs out of cards.
Count your pairs.
Whoever has the most wins!

Remember, hold your
cards up so no
one else can
see them!

35

GAME #4: CRAZY EIGHTS

Number of players: 2, 3, or 4

When is an eight not an eight?

In Crazy Eights!

Everyone can be a magician

in this wacky game.

Don't worry.
You'll see what that
means in a minute.

First, deal eight cards to each player.

Place the rest of the cards in a stack

in the middle of the table.

Take the top card off

flip!

the stack and lay

it face up

beside the stack.

In this game, players hold

their cards in fans.

If you are the dealer,
you get to go first.

I go first!
Me, me, me!!!

Look at the card in the middle
of the table.
You must play one of your cards
on top of it.
But you can't play just any old card.
Your card must match that card.
It must either be the same number
or the same suit.

Uh-oh! You have no cards that work.
You will have to draw cards
from the stack
until you get one that you can play.

Sometimes you'll be holding
a lot of cards in your hand.
Don't worry. Slowly but surely,
you'll get rid of them!

But wait!
Do you have an eight? *Any* eight?
This is what Crazy Eights is all about!
If you have an eight in your hand, or
if you draw one from the deck,
you can play it.

You can also make it any suit.
If you have a lot of clubs to play,
say, "This eight is clubs," even if the
eight is a diamond.

Thank goodness for magic eights!

Presto!

What if the middle stack
runs out of cards?
Then the dealer picks up the stack
of face-up cards. He leaves the
top card face-up on the table and
shuffles the rest of the pack.

These form the new pile to draw from.
Who wins? The first player to run
out of cards!

Watch out! It's hard to STOP
playing Crazy Eights
once you start!

CLOCK SOLITAIRE

GAME #5:

CLOCK SOLITAIRE

Number of players: 1

Are you all by yourself?

Do you still want to play cards?

Some games work for one player.

These are called Solitaire.

Start with a simple Solitaire game called Clock.

After shuffling the cards,
deal them into 13 face-down piles.
Twelve piles should form a circle
like the numbers on a clock.
Put the last pile in the middle.
There will be four cards in each pile.
Now turn up the top card
of the middle pile.
Where does it belong?
If it is a seven,
it goes at seven o'clock.

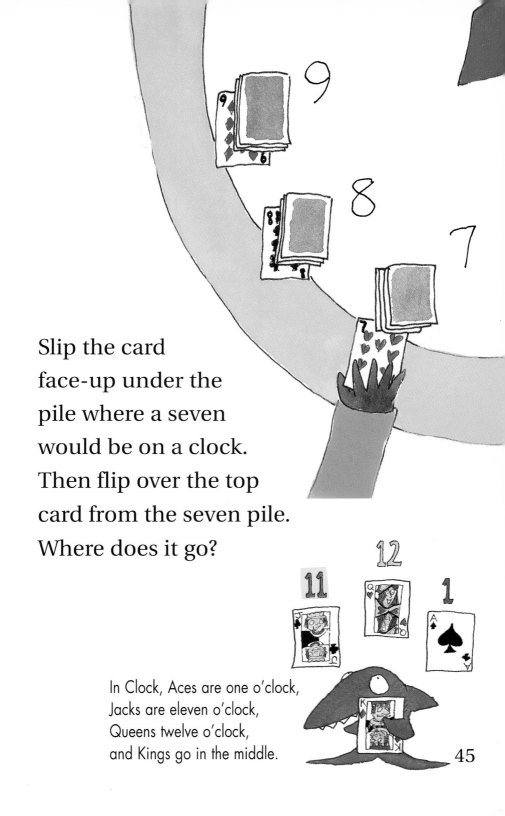

Slip the card face-up under the pile where a seven would be on a clock. Then flip over the top card from the seven pile. Where does it go?

In Clock, Aces are one o'clock, Jacks are eleven o'clock, Queens twelve o'clock, and Kings go in the middle.

45

Keep sliding cards under and
taking cards off the tops of piles.
When you get to the last
face-down cards,
the numbers on the clock
face will appear.
But watch out for the Kings!
If all four of them reach
the center before the other
piles are done, the game ends.
It's time to deal out another clock!

You're sunk!
You're FIN-ished!

Now you know how to play
a few card games.
Ask your family and friends
to teach you more.
Then you will become
a card shark, too!

Bye!